Rosie
the Honey Bear
Fairy

With magical love to Lara

Special thanks to Rachel Elliot

If you purchased this book without a cover, you should be aware
that this book is stolen property. It was reported as "unsold and
destroyed" to the publisher, and neither the author nor the
publisher has received any payment for this "stripped book."

No part of this work may be reproduced, stored in a retrieval
system, or transmitted in any form or by any means, electronic,
mechanical, photocopying, recording, or otherwise, without written
permission of the publisher. For information regarding permission,
write to Rainbow Magic Limited c/o HIT Entertainment,
830 South Greenville Avenue, Allen, TX 75002-3320.

ISBN 978-0-545-70855-5

Copyright © 2013 by Rainbow Magic Limited.

All rights reserved. Published by Scholastic Inc., 557 Broadway, New
York, NY 10012, by arrangement with Rainbow Magic Limited.

SCHOLASTIC and associated logos are trademarks and/or
registered trademarks of Scholastic Inc. RAINBOW MAGIC
is a trademark of Rainbow Magic Limited. Reg. U.S. Patent &
Trademark Office and other countries. HIT and the HIT logo are
trademarks of HIT Entertainment Limited.

12 11 10 9 8 7 6 5 4 3 2 1   15 16 17 18 19/0

Printed in the U.S.A.   40

First Scholastic printing, January 2015

Rosie the honey bear
fairy
33305233701881
0jpb   08/03/15

Rosie
the Honey Bear Fairy

by Daisy Meadows

SCHOLASTIC INC.

I love animals—yes, I do,
I want my very own private zoo!
I'll capture all the animals one by one,
With fairy magic to help me get it done!

A koala, a tiger, an Arctic fox,
I'll keep them in cages with giant locks.
Every kind of animal will be there,
A panda, a meerkat, a honey bear.
The animals will be my property,
I'll be master of my own menagerie!

Contents

Bees and Butterflies

"I wish it could be summer all year long," cheered Kirsty Tate.

She straightened up from filling her wheelbarrow and smiled at her best friend, Rachel Walker. Rachel dropped a small shovel into her own wheelbarrow and smiled back at Kirsty.

"Me too," she said, her cheeks pink from all her hard work. "And I wish we could help out at the nature reserve for longer, too. I love the animals so much!"

The girls were spending a week of their summer vacation helping at Wild Woods Nature Reserve as part of a team of junior rangers. Every day, they earned badges for their backpacks by doing special tasks. Becky, the head of the nature reserve, planned the tasks. That morning, she had thought of something especially fun for them to do together.

"I'd like you to plant shrubs along the bank of the stream," she had said. "The shrubs will attract bees and butterflies to the nature reserve. We depend on them to help keep the plants alive."

The girls had filled their wheelbarrows

with pots of flowering shrubs, spades, short shovels, forks, and watering cans.

"We're ready, Becky!" called Kirsty.

"All right," Becky replied with a grin. "Follow me!"

She led them through the woods, and the wheelbarrows bumped over the branches and pinecones on the ground.

When they came out of the woods, the stream was straight ahead. Next to the clear, sparkling water they saw a row of little wooden houses on platforms.

"They look like fairy houses," said Kirsty excitedly.

She had spoken quietly, but Becky heard her and laughed.

"Yes," she said. "If
fairies existed, I bet
they'd love to live
in one of these cute
houses! Actually,
they're beehives.
The bees will use
the nectar from the
flowers you're planting
to make honey."

Rachel and Kirsty smiled at each
other. They had a secret that bonded
them as best friends forever. They knew
that fairies really did exist, and they
had often visited Fairyland and shared
adventures with their fairy friends. During
their most recent visit, the fairies had even
given them the ability to understand
what animals were saying.

Becky led the girls to a little stone bridge that crossed the stream.

"I'd like you to plant some shrubs on both sides of the stream, close to the bridge," she said. "Do you know how to plant them?"

"Yes," said Rachel. "My mom loves gardening, and I've helped her lots of times."

"Great," said Becky. "I'll leave you to it. Call me if you need any help, and have fun!"

As Becky walked away, Rachel pulled on her gardening gloves and Kirsty looked around the area.

"Let's start on this side of the bridge," Kirsty suggested.

"Yes, and I think I'll plant a shrub with pink flowers first," said Rachel. "What about you?"

"Blue!" said Kirsty, picking a pretty little plant out of her wheelbarrow. "Let's get digging!"

They picked up their shovels and started to dig two holes. After a short while, a group of colorful butterflies fluttered toward them. As they hovered over the holes, the girls heard a babble of tiny, curious voices.

"What are they doing?"

"Why is she opening up the ground?"

"What's going on?"

Rachel laughed and paused, resting one foot on the shoulder of her shovel.

"Hello, butterflies," she said. "We're planting some flowering shrubs so you'll want to come back here."

"That's wonderful!" twittered the butterflies all together. "Thank you! Thank you!"

Suddenly, among the wafting wings of the butterflies, Kirsty spotted a flash of blue sparkling in the sunlight.

"Oh, is that a fairy?" she asked in excitement.

Rachel whipped her head around to look where Kirsty was pointing. She squinted her eyes to see in the bright sunlight, and then shook her head.

"It's a big blue dragonfly," she said. "But even so, I have a funny feeling . . ."

"Me too," said Kirsty. "Like there's magic nearby!"

Under the Bridge

Rachel and Kirsty kept digging, watched closely by the butterflies. They knew that if there was magic around, it would find them when the time was right.

As they worked, the girls thought about the busy week they were having. As well as helping at Wild Woods Nature Reserve, they were also helping the

Baby Animal Rescue Fairies. Animals all around the world needed to be protected from Jack Frost and his pesky goblins.

On their first day at the nature reserve in Kirsty's town, the two friends had met Bertram, a frog footman from Fairyland. He was visiting relatives at the pond. He had then whisked the girls away to the nature reserve in Fairyland. There they had spent time with the Baby Animal Rescue Fairies, who looked after animals in both Fairyland and in the human world. But Jack Frost and his goblins had been up to no good again. Jack had decided that he liked animals so much, he wanted to collect one of each kind for his own private zoo—no matter what!

Kirsty and Rachel tried to tell Jack Frost that animals weren't like collectible

toys. They needed
lots of care! But
he sneered at
them and stole
the Baby Animal
Rescue Fairies'
magic key
chains,  which helped them protect the
animals. Jack gave the magic charms to
his goblins and ordered them to steal
some animals from the human world for
his zoo. All animals were now in danger!

The seven fairies had given Kirsty and
Rachel the power to talk to animals
when they offered to protect them. They
had already saved five baby animals.
Would they need to help the Baby
Animal Rescue Fairies save some more
today?

As they planted the shrubs, the girls wondered about the adventures they might have. The butterflies fluttered closer and closer.

"It's going to be so nice to have some beautiful plants to visit around here," said a large red Admiral butterfly, very close to Kirsty's ear.

"Oh, your wings are tickling my cheek!" Kirsty giggled.

"I apologize," said the butterfly, moving away at once. "We're very excited to see all the changes that the young people have been making."

"Me too," added the blue dragonfly.

"I've been flying all over the nature reserve. You junior rangers are doing a great job. Thank you!"

"Can you hear something buzzing?" asked Kirsty as she took her shrub out of its pot.

"It's the bees!" The butterflies began to twitter among themselves. "Now we'll have some fun!"

Kirsty felt a little bit nervous when a dark cloud of bees swarmed around them, but they soon put her at ease.

"New flowers?"

"For us?"

"Wonderful!"

"We're buzzing with excitement!"

The insects swooped over the water and turned somersaults in the air as the girls planted shrub after shrub in the ground.

"I'm going to start on the other side of the stream," said Kirsty at last. Rachel nodded.

Kirsty selected a pot and started to walk over the bridge. Halfway across, she paused and bent down to pick up a twig. She stood up and dropped it into the gurgling stream. Then she rushed to the other side to watch it float out from under the bridge.

"Let's race!" said Rachel, who had been watching her best friend.

Rachel pulled off her gloves and each girl chose a twig. They dropped the twigs into the water and then hung over the other side of the bridge to see who would win. The insects watched and cheered as Kirsty's twig edged into the lead. Then, suddenly, Rachel spotted something strange in the water.

"Look at that leaf," she said. "Does it look *different* to you?"

She pointed to a small leaf that was floating downstream toward the bridge. It was glowing!

The bees flew down to the leaf, and then zoomed back to the girls in a happy swarm.

"It's not a leaf!" they buzzed. "It's Rosie the Honey Bear Fairy!"

Surprise in a Hive

The girls hung over the side of the bridge and watched Rosie fly up to them. She perched on the stone bridge and gave Rachel and Kirsty a big smile. She was wearing a sparkly blue top and light blue jeans. Her honey-blond hair was tousled.

"It looks like you're having fun!" she said. "I'm sorry, but I'm here to drag you away from your game. A baby bear is missing, and I really need your help to find him. Will you come with me?"

"Of course we'll come," said Rachel and Kirsty together.

Rosie winked and waved her wand in a circle above her head, making a hoop of sparkling fairy dust. It grew wider and wider, until it surrounded the girls and whisked them away at once.

They blinked, and found themselves looking down over a lush wooded valley. There were tall trees all around them, and the leaves were rustling in the gentle breeze. The ground was soft with layers of mulched leaves and twigs.

"Hello, Mama Bear," said Rosie in a gentle voice.

The girls looked around and saw an

enormous brown bear sitting on a rock
in a clearing. She was holding a dripping
honeycomb in her paw, but she wasn't
eating it. They stepped closer and saw
that tears were trickling down her
furry cheeks.

"What's the matter?" asked Kirsty,
putting her hand on the bear's furry paw.
"Can we help you?"

"It's my baby, Billy," said Mama Bear with a little sob. "He's missing!"

The girls exchanged a suspicious glance.

"I'm sure the goblins are behind this," Rachel said.

"If they are, I promise we'll stop them," Kirsty told Mama Bear. "We'll find your little Billy and bring him home safe and sound."

Just then, a bee buzzed out from behind Mama Bear's head.

"Billy's missing?" he exclaimed, sounding upset. "He's my friend! How can I help?"

"Have you seen anything unusual in the valley?" Kirsty asked. "Like strange green creatures?"

"The Queen Bee might know something," said the little bee. "If you follow me, I'll take you to her right away!"

Rachel and Kirsty turned to Rosie. If they were going to visit the Queen Bee, they were going to have to be fairy-size. With a flick of her wand, Rosie transformed the girls into fairies. Now that they were tiny, they could see the kind expression on the bee's furry face.

His wings made a loud, whirring sound, and created a breeze that fanned the girls' faces. He gave them a little smile.

"Follow me," he said. "I'll take you to the Queen Bee."

"We'll be back as soon as we can, Mama Bear," said Rosie.

They waved to the sad-faced bear, and then followed the little bee up to the top of a tree, where his hive was nestled among green leaves.

It looked like a small city towering above them.

The bee led them to the entrance, where two guard bees were hovering.

"These are my guests," said the bee. "They want to visit the Queen Bee."

"Welcome to our hive," said the guard bees.

The girls followed their friend into the straw-colored lower chamber. The walls were full of honeycomb cells. The Queen Bee was sitting on her throne in the center of the chamber. She was surrounded by drone bees, who were combing her fur and polishing her wings.

Rachel and Kirsty gasped. They recognized that royal fuzzy face!

"It's Queenie!" said Rachel, flitting forward to greet their old friend.

The last time they had seen Queenie, she was living with the Rainbow Fairies in the pot at the end of the rainbow.

"Rachel! Kirsty!" Queenie exclaimed. "How nice to see you!"

"You, too," said Kirsty. "But we thought you were living with the Rainbow Fairies."

"I had a lovely time there," said Queenie, "but I missed the other bees. So now I'm the queen of this hive. Come, dear girls, sit yourselves down, have some nectar, and tell me what brings you here."

Noisy Hikers

The drone bees brought acorn cups full
of delicious nectar. Rachel and Kirsty
sipped their drinks and talked with
Queenie about the old adventures they'd
had together with the Rainbow Fairies.
Then they told her about how Billy the
little bear was missing.

"I'm very sorry to hear that," said
Queenie. "Billy is very sweet, and all the
bees love him."

"Excuse me, Your Majesty," said one of the drone bees. "The park ranger knows everything that happens in the valley. Perhaps he's seen something unusual that will help these fairies find little Billy?"

"Excellent idea," said Queenie.

The girls finished their drinks and stood up. Queenie nodded to two of her drone bees, and they buzzed forward carrying a scrumptious-looking piece of honeycomb.

"Share that with Billy when you find him," said Queenie. "It's been lovely to see you again, girls."

She commanded a swarm of bees to
lead them to the park ranger. Rosie,
Kirsty, and Rachel zoomed along behind
the bees as they weaved their way
among the trees.

At last they heard the sound of a man
whistling up ahead.

"That's the park ranger!" said their bee
friends. "Good luck!"

As the bees buzzed away, Kirsty and
Rachel fluttered down and landed
behind a bush. Hovering above them,
Rosie waved her wand and turned
them back into humans.

"OK," said Rachel. "Let's find out
what that park ranger knows."

She tucked the honeycomb into her
backpack. Rosie jumped in, too, glad to
rest her wings. They tramped through
the woods, following the sound of the
whistling. The park ranger stood on a
grassy hill overlooking the wooded
valley.

"Excuse me?" Kirsty called.

The park ranger whirled around. He
had a friendly tanned face and spiky
brown hair.

"Hello!" he said. "What can I do
for you?"

"We were just wondering if you had
seen anything unusual in the valley
today?" Kirsty asked. "We're . . . um . . .
looking for someone."

The park ranger nodded.

"There was a group of noisy hikers
here earlier," he said. "I had to warn
them to be quiet because they could scare
the wildlife."

Rachel squeezed Kirsty's hand.

"What did they look like?" she asked.

"They looked a little silly to be honest," the park ranger said with a chuckle. "They were wearing bright green hiking gear with the biggest hiking boots I've ever seen, and one of them had a backpack that was stuffed full. Are they friends of yours?"

"Not exactly," said Kirsty, gritting her teeth.

"Do you know where they went?" Rachel asked.

The park ranger pointed to a curving path that led down through the woods.

"That leads to the river at the bottom of the valley," he said. "That's where they were heading. You might still catch them if you're quick."

"Thank you!" said Rachel. "Come on, Kirsty. Let's go!"

She set off down the path, with Kirsty close behind her. They broke into a jog, and Rosie held on tight to the inside of Rachel's backpack. It was hard to run in the hot midday sun, but they had to stop the goblins.

With a final curve, the path came to
an end next to a large, meandering river.
Rachel held out her arm to stop Kirsty.

"Look, there they are!" she said.

There were three goblins on the other
side of the river, pushing one another and
squabbling. On the ground between
them was a small raft.

"There's a bridge!" said Kirsty, pointing downstream. "Come on!"

The girls ran down the riverbank and raced over the stone bridge to the opposite bank. The goblins turned and scowled at them.

"What are you doing here?"

"Pesky humans!"

"Leave us alone!"

There was no sign of Billy. Rachel put her hands on her hips.

"What have you done with the bear cub?" she asked.

The goblins glanced at one another.

"Don't know what you're talking about,"  said the first goblin, turning very red in the face.

"You're lying," Kirsty stated, folding her arms across her chest.

"Prove it!" said the second goblin.

The third goblin stuck out his very long tongue and blew a loud raspberry.

"Billy *must* be here somewhere," said Rachel.

"And my magic key chain, too," Rosie added, sticking her head out of Rachel's backpack.

"But *where*?" asked Kirsty.

Branching Out

Just then, one of the goblins started to push the raft into the water, turning his back to the girls. Now they could see the enormous green backpack that the park ranger had mentioned. As he had said, it was packed full.

"What could the goblins need that would fill such a big bag?" Rachel wondered aloud.

Suddenly, the backpack seemed to wriggle.

"It moved!" cried Rosie. "Girls, the backpack moved!"

"I saw it, too," said Kirsty.

As they watched, a furry little snout poked out of the top of the backpack. It was followed by a pair of shining brown eyes and two fuzzy ears.

"It's Billy!" exclaimed Rosie.

"Look, he has your magic key chain," Rachel added with a smile.

Billy had pushed one paw out of the

bag, and he was holding on tight to a
fluffy key chain in the shape of a bear.

The girls dashed forward to try to keep
the goblins from getting away. But two
of them were already on board. Just
as Rachel and Kirsty reached the water's
edge, the third goblin jumped onto
the raft, too. It slid out of reach, and the
goblins laughed as they floated away.

With one swift wave of Rosie's wand, Rachel and Kirsty were fairies again.

"Let's fly among the trees on the riverbank," Rosie suggested. "Let them think that they left us behind."

The girls zoomed along, darting between the trees and keeping level with the little raft. It was bobbing up and down on the fast-moving water.

Suddenly, Rachel gave a cry.

"Billy's climbing out of the backpack!" she exclaimed.

The goblins hadn't noticed that Billy was free. Just then, Rachel saw a fallen branch jutting out of the water.

"Oh, no!" she cried. "The raft's heading straight toward that branch!"

The raft wobbled and then veered around the branch. The girls let out sighs of relief.

"That gives me an idea," said Kirsty. "Remember that stone bridge farther downstream? We need to get there before the raft does!"

Rachel, Kirsty, and Rosie zoomed to the bridge as fast as they could. As they flew, Kirsty explained her plan.

"We just have to hope that Billy Bear really loves honey!" she said with a smile.

When they reached the bridge, Rosie turned the girls into humans again. Then she used her magic to bring the fallen branch from the river to the bridge. Rachel dug into her backpack and pulled out the honeycomb that Queenie had given them earlier.

"Rub the honey all over the branch," said Kirsty. "Quickly!"

Rachel covered the branch in honey, and then the girls dangled it over the edge of the bridge, holding on to the top end.

"I hope Billy Bear sees it!" said Kirsty.

"Please let him be hungry for some honey!" Rachel added.

Their plan was ready—all it needed was for Billy to play his part!

Just then, the goblin raft floated around the bend in the river. It was bobbing along with Billy on the back, but the magic charm was no longer dangling from his paw.

"Where did my magic key chain go?" asked Rosie.

There was no time to find out the answer—the raft was about to pass under the bridge!

Billy noticed the honey
dripping from the
branch, and
reached up to it.
He began to lick
the honey with
his long tongue,
and he started to
climb the log.

"Yes, Billy!"
called Rachel. "Good
bear! Keep coming!"

She and Kirsty held on tight to the
branch, taking on the weight of the bear.
Below, the goblins squawked in dismay
and clutched at the sides of the stone
bridge, trying to slow the raft down.

"No, Billy!" shouted the goblin with
the backpack. "Bad bear! Come back!"

"Billy!" called another goblin. "Look here, Billy!"

The goblin held up the magic key chain, which he knew would lure the cub back. Billy looked over and then started to slide back down the branch.

"No, come back!" Kirsty cried. "Billy!"

The little bear reached out one paw to get the key chain. The goblin jerked his hand backward, and sent the honey-bear charm flying into the river!

Bees, Bears, and Badges

Rosie swooped down after the key chain, and the goblin jumped into the water with a loud belly flop. Rachel and Kirsty watched Rosie dive into the river, but they couldn't do anything to help. Billy was climbing up the honey-covered branch again, and the girls needed all their strength to hold on to it.

It seemed to take forever before Billy's little paws were in reach, but at last Rachel was able to grasp them and pull him up to safety. The girls gave him a big hug.

"We're going to take you home to your mama," Kirsty told him.

"What about Rosie?" asked Rachel, holding Billy while he finished the honey.

At that moment, Rosie flew up from
the other side of the bridge. She shook off
sparkling drops of river water and gave a
whoop of triumph.

"I got it!" she
cried happily.

Rachel and
Kirsty grinned
when they saw
that she was
holding her key
chain. It had
magically shrunk to
fairy-size, and it was back
where it belonged at last.

"We did it!" said Rosie, hovering next
to the girls and Billy.

"What about the goblins?" Rachel
asked.

They all leaned over the bridge and saw a dripping–wet goblin being hauled back onto the raft.

"You two are going to be in big trouble with Jack Frost. What will he say when we get back without the bear cub?" he snarled at the other goblins.

"You were the one who dropped the magic key chain!" snapped the second goblin.

"We're *all* going to be locked up in the dungeon!" wailed the third goblin.

The raft floated away down the river, and the sound of the goblins' bickering traveled across the water. The girls could hear it even after the raft disappeared from sight.

"Come on," said Rosie. "Let's get this little cub back to his mama."

The girls hiked back the way they had come, up the winding path that led out of the valley. Rachel and Kirsty took turns carrying Billy, and Rosie dangled her charm in front of him to keep him happy.

They went back through the woods, and at last they reached the clearing where Mama Bear was still sitting on the rock.

When she saw her baby, Mama Bear's eyes filled with happy tears. She lumbered over to him, scooped him into her arms, and hugged him tightly.

"I've missed you, little one," she whispered in an amazingly gentle voice.

Billy gave her a snuffly kiss, and she

pressed a honeycomb treat into his paw.
Then she looked up at the girls.

"How can I ever thank you?" she
asked.

"We're just glad that Billy's back where
he belongs," said Rachel.

The cub held out his arms toward her,
and she let him give her a little bear hug.
Kirsty got a hug, too.
They were about
to say good-bye
when there
was a loud
buzzing
noise. It
was a huge
swarm of
bees. Between
them, they were

carrying two little walnut shells filled with honey.

One bee buzzed to the front of the swarm and the girls saw that it was the one they had met here earlier.

"Our beloved queen has sent you this gift," he said. "As a thank you for finding our friend Billy, please accept this honey. It's some of our very best!"

"Thank you very much," said Rachel, taking one of the shells.

"Please give Queenie our love," Kirsty added, taking the other shell.

While the bees gave them three cheers, Rosie waved her wand and transported the girls back to Wild Woods. Rachel let out a happy sigh and gazed around. Then her eyes fell on her wheelbarrow.

"Oh my goodness!" she exclaimed. "We haven't finished planting the shrubs yet."

"Let's get to work," said Kirsty.

The bees and butterflies were still flitting around the colorful flowers, and several more beautiful blue dragonflies had joined them. Rosie went to greet them, and had fun playing while Rachel and Kirsty finished planting their shrubs.

At last the work was done. The girls filled their watering cans from the clear stream and watered each plant. Then they sat down on the bank and rested.

"It's beautiful here," said Rosie, landing on Rachel's knee. "It reminds me of the nature reserve in Fairyland. And these flowers smell wonderful."

"The honey we make from the nectar will be absolutely delicious," said a bee as he circled around Kirsty's head. "I can't wait!"

"Ooh, someone's coming!" said a little white butterfly in a panic. "Hide, Rosie!"

With a good-bye
wave, Rosie
flew onto a blue
flower and hid
among the petals.
Then the girls saw
Becky striding toward
them from the woods. She looked at
the planting they had done and smiled.

"Excellent work, both of you," she
said. "These look perfect. You've
definitely earned your badges today."

From one of the big pockets in her
cargo shorts, she drew out two flower-
shaped badges. As she handed them to
Rachel and Kirsty, a bee zoomed under
her nose.

"The flowers are already attracting lots
of insects," she said.

"And a fairy, too," said Rachel in a tiny whisper.

She and Kirsty looked over at the blue flower where Rosie was hiding and squeezed each other's hands. They had really enjoyed their adventure with Rosie. But there was still one magic key chain to find. They hoped that they would meet Nora the Arctic Fox Fairy tomorrow!

Rachel and Kirsty found Mae, Kitty,
Mara, Savannah, Kimberly, and
Rosie's missing magic key chains.
Now it's time for them to help

Nora
the Arctic Fox Fairy!

Join their next adventure in this special
sneak peek . . .

Moonlight Magic

"Isn't it a beautiful evening?" Rachel Walker remarked to her best friend, Kirsty Tate. They stared up at the night sky dotted with tiny, glittering stars. The evening air was warm and still, and above the trees the moon shone with a pale, silvery light.

"It's a perfect way to end our week at Wild Woods," Kirsty agreed. The girls had volunteered to spend part of their summer vacation at the nature reserve near Kirsty's home, learning how to be junior rangers. Now it was their last day, and all the volunteers were waiting outside the wildlife center for Becky, the head of Wild Woods, to join them for a special evening.

"It's really nice of Becky to take us on a moonlit walk," Rachel said. "I hope we see lots of different animals."

"Becky said it was a special treat because we'd all worked so hard," Kirsty reminded her. "Even though we also have our badges as proof!"

Both girls gazed proudly at the pockets of their backpacks, which were covered with badges. Every time they'd completed their tasks successfully, Becky had given them a badge, and the girls had six so far.

There was a murmur of excitement as Becky hurried out of the wildlife center, carrying a bag of equipment.

"We have a wonderful evening for our walk," Becky said. "But to make the most of it, you'll all need one of *these*!" She took a flashlight out of the bag and turned it on. Rachel and Kirsty were surprised to see the flashlight glow red. "These flashlights have special red filters that allow you to see in the dark," Becky went on, handing the flashlights out. "But they won't disturb wildlife like a bright yellow beam would. So keep your eyes peeled for animals that only come out at night!"

"And we should keep our eyes peeled for fairies, too!" Kirsty whispered to Rachel excitedly.

RAINBOW magic™

Which Magical Fairies Have You Met?

- ☐ The Rainbow Fairies
- ☐ The Weather Fairies
- ☐ The Jewel Fairies
- ☐ The Pet Fairies
- ☐ The Dance Fairies
- ☐ The Music Fairies
- ☐ The Sports Fairies
- ☐ The Party Fairies
- ☐ The Ocean Fairies
- ☐ The Night Fairies
- ☐ The Magical Animal Fairies
- ☐ The Princess Fairies
- ☐ The Superstar Fairies
- ☐ The Fashion Fairies
- ☐ The Sugar & Spice Fairies
- ☐ The Earth Fairies
- ☐ The Magical Crafts Fairies

■ SCHOLASTIC

SCHOLASTIC and associated logos are trademarks and/or registered trademarks of Scholastic Inc. © 2015 Rainbow Magic Limited. HIT and the HIT Entertainment logo are trademarks of HIT Entertainment Limited.

Find all of your favorite fairy friends at
scholastic.com/rainbowmagic

HiT entertainment

RMFAIRY

RAINBOW magic™

SPECIAL EDITION

Which Magical Fairies Have You Met?

3 stories in each one!

- Joy the Summer Vacation Fairy
- Holly the Christmas Fairy
- Kylie the Carnival Fairy
- Stella the Star Fairy
- Shannon the Ocean Fairy
- Trixie the Halloween Fairy
- Gabriella the Snow Kingdom Fairy
- Juliet the Valentine Fairy
- Mia the Bridesmaid Fairy
- Flora the Dress-Up Fairy
- Paige the Christmas Play Fairy
- Emma the Easter Fairy
- Cara the Camp Fairy
- Destiny the Rock Star Fairy
- Belle the Birthday Fairy
- Olympia the Games Fairy
- Selena the Sleepover Fairy
- Cheryl the Christmas Tree Fairy
- Florence the Friendship Fairy
- Lindsay the Luck Fairy
- Brianna the Tooth Fairy
- Autumn the Falling Leaves Fairy
- Keira the Movie Star Fairy
- Addison the April Fool's Day Fairy
- Bailey the Babysitter Fairy
- Natalie the Christmas Stocking Fairy
- Lila and Myla the Twins Fairies

■ SCHOLASTIC

SCHOLASTIC and associated logos are trademarks and/or registered trademarks of Scholastic Inc. © 2015 Rainbow Magic Limited. HIT and the HIT Entertainment logo are trademarks of HIT Entertainment Limited.

Find all of your favorite fairy friends at
scholastic.com/rainbowmagic

HIT entertainment

RMSPECIAL14

RAINBOW magic

These activities are magical!
Play dress-up, send friendship notes, and much more!

HIT and the HIT Entertainment logo are
trademarks of HIT Entertainment Limited.
© 2010 Rainbow Magic Limited.
SCHOLASTIC and associated logos are trademarks
and/or registered trademarks of Scholastic Inc.

■SCHOLASTIC
www.scholastic.com
www.rainbowmagiconline.com

HiT entertainment

RMACTIV.